When I Close My Eyes

Al Cerrar Mis Ojos

by Phillip D. Cortez   Illustrated by Nacho Garcia

Very special thanks to my parents, Mom and Honey, a couple of dreamers who were told that they'd never have children of their own...

For my brothers Steven, Michael, Paul and Mark; Each of us undoubtedly made my parents wish the doctors were right from time to time...

And for my wife, Patty, and our children: Ivan, Cameron, Ava and Zoe. They're my daily reminders that dreams do come true.

© 2013 Phillip D. Cortez

Illustrated by Nacho Garcia. Translated by Bertha Peña. Designers and Team MVPs: Claudia Cornejo, Javier Guzman, Richard Nicholson & Veronica Lucero

Published in 2013 by Monkey C Publishing
El Paso, Texas

ISBN: 978-0-615-87483-8

  This project was inspired by my late cousin, Jared. He was a kid that wasn't supposed to live a day much less five years, but the courage he displayed during his short life is something I will never forget.

Jared had Cerebral Palsy, which made it extremely difficult for him to talk, yet there was so much going on inside that head of his, behind those big brown eyes.

When I Close My Eyes is full of the imagery that I would have wished for Jared to see whenever he closed his eyes - and what I prayed he may have seen in Heaven.

This is for all the dreamers out there - and for those working hard every day to make those dreams a reality.

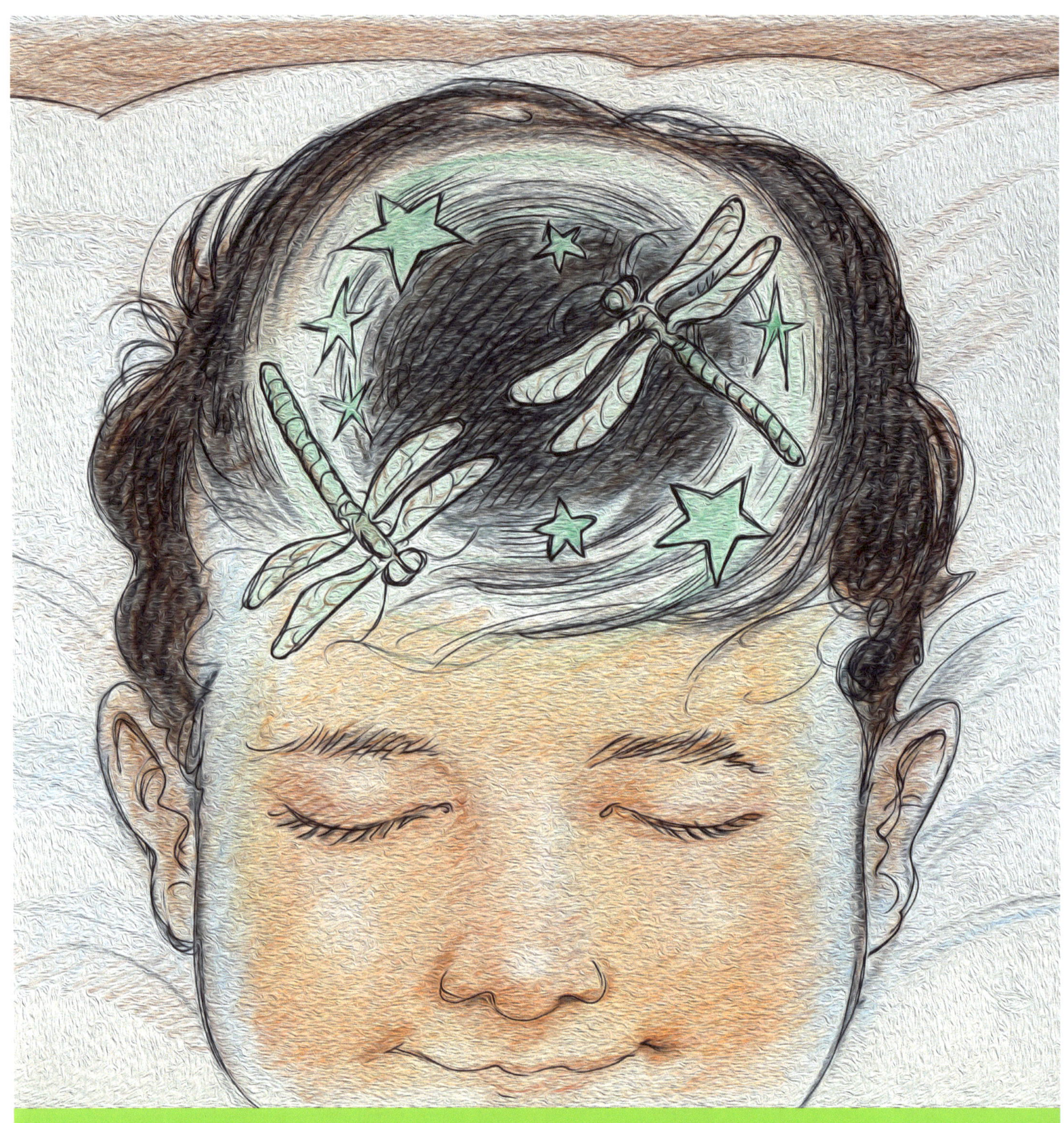

When I close my eyes tightly, I see
Little green stars that whirl around
Like dragonflies inside my head.

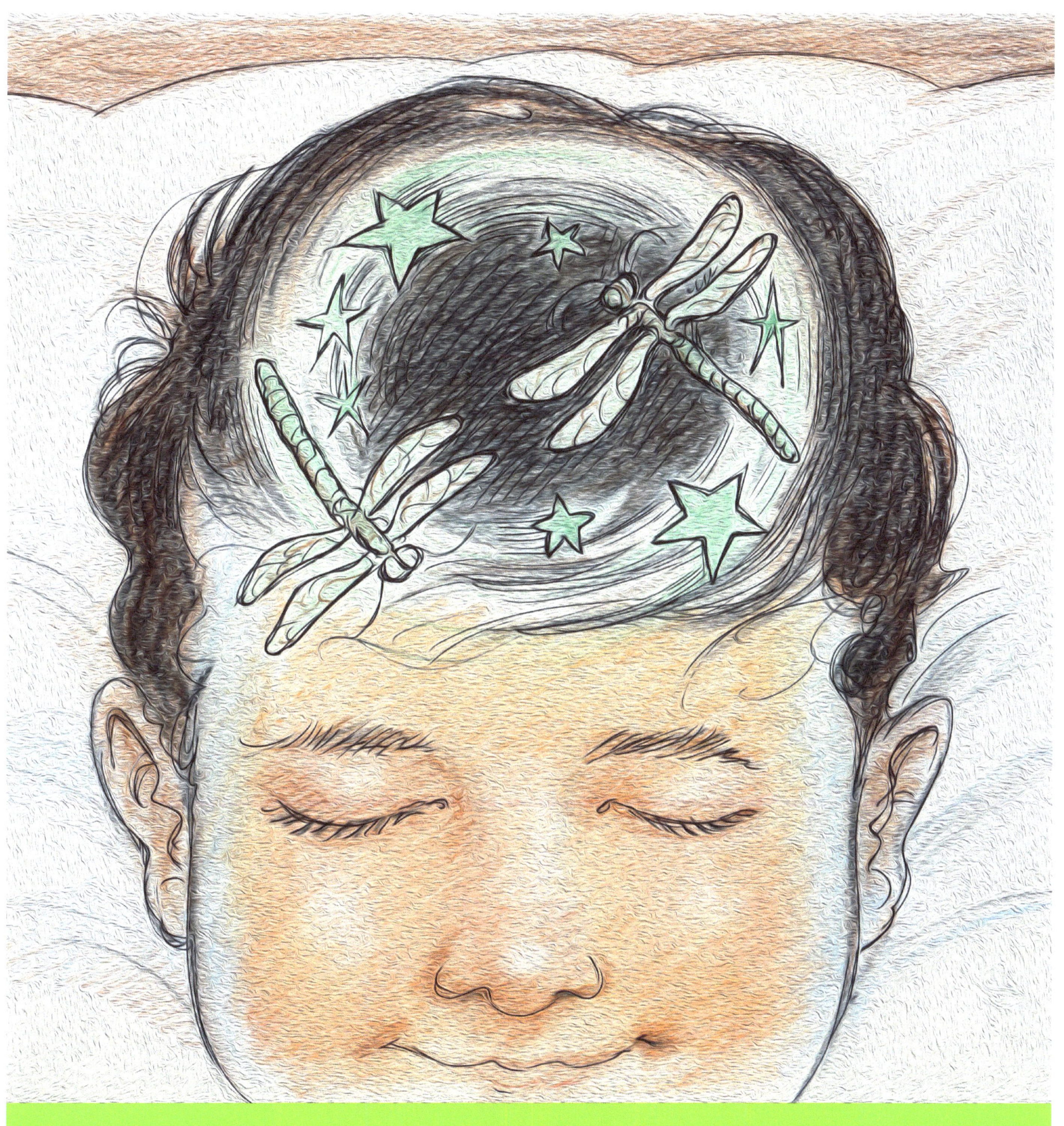

Al cerrar mis ojos, veo
Pequeñas estrellas verdes
Que giran alrededor de mi cabeza
como libélulas.

If I close my eyes tighter
Dragonflies turn to snowflakes
That fall like floating feathers
From a pillow fight!

Si aprieto mis ojos
Las libélulas se convierten en copos de nieve
Que caen como hojas flotantes
Causadas por una pelea de almohadas.

When I close my eyes I become
anything;
An eagle that skies through cotton
candy clouds
And swoops back to Earth in a single
flight...

Al cerrar mis ojos, me convierto en lo
que sea;
En el águila que aletea por las nubes
echas de algodón azucarado
Que luego se apresura a la Tierra de
un solo vuelo...

U.S.A.

A space traveler
discovering new worlds
In a rocket ship
surrounded by a sea of
night.

En viajero del espacio que
descubre mundos nuevos
En una nave espacial
rodeada del mar de la
oscura noche.

When I close my eyes,
walking home alone
From the bus stop isn't all
that bad...

**Al cerrar mis ojos, el
caminar solo a casa
Desde la parada del
autobús, no está nada
mal...**

THIS END
UP

And my best friend Diego
can stay and play until dark
Without his *abuelita* getting
mad.

Y mi mejor amigo Diego
se puede quedar a jugar
hasta que anochezca
Sin que su *grandma* se
enoje.

When I close my eyes, I'm
a superhero
Who fights for all that is
good...

Al cerrar mis ojos, soy un
superhéroe
Que lucha por todo lo
bueno...

Or a ship's captain on
the wild, wild sea
Sailing over waves of
blueberry punch.

O el capitán del barco
en el mar salvaje
Navegando sobre olas
de jugo de arándanos.

And Diego is my first mate;
together we sail
Through storms of lemon
drop candy
That pours from cracks in
piñata-shaped clouds;
Tangerine gulls fly over
chocolate mountains.

Y Diego es mi primer
compañero; juntos
navegamos
Por medio de tormentas de
gotas de dulce limón
Que caen por las rajaduras
de nubes que parecen
piñatas;
Gaviotas color naranja
vuelan sobre montañas de
chocolate.

But when I open my eyes,
I am still me,
A little boy from the Sun City
Who likes to run barefoot on
the cool green grass.

Pero al abrir mis ojos,
aún soy yo,
El pequeño niño de la
Ciudad del Sol
A quien le gusta correr descalzo
sobre el pasto verde.

Me and **Diego** play make-
believe
Until the sun goes down;
Our shadows are ten feet
tall!

It's time to go inside now.
Off to bed I go,
To close my eyes…

Yo y **Diego** jugamos,
fingimos
Hasta que el sol se pone;
¡Nuestras sombras miden
diez pies!

Es hora de irnos a casa
Y a dormir me voy,
A cerrar mis ojos…

…and dream.

…y soñar.

Phillip D. Cortez

Photo by Mayra Silerio mayra sileriophotography.com

As a kid from El Paso, Texas, Phillip Cortez found himself fascinated by books and stories and the people who told them. So he made a crucial decision in grade school that one day he was going to take his love for reading and become a storyteller, too.

"I was always making up stories to try and get out of trouble anyway," he laughs. "But that sort of comes with the territory when you've got four brothers."

Cortez began his career as a freelance sports writer, writing stories for his local paper and later moving onto writing editorials and feature stories for different publications. His children's book, "Night Rhythms," was published in 2011 and a collection of short stories and essays for young adults is scheduled to be released in the summer 2014.

Nacho Garcia

Born and raised in El Paso, Texas, Nacho L. Garcia, Jr. earned his Bachelor of Fine Arts degree from the University of Texas - El Paso in 1971.

"My love for any kind of illustration and design has enabled me to work in advertising, graphic design and commercial illustration for the last 32 years," he said. "Just rcently I have found a new avenue for my artistic outlet, children's book illustration."

When he's not illustrating "Nacho Toons," his popular popular political cartoon that often appears in the El Paso Times, Garcia is working in his home studio painting commissioned portraits and framed caricatures.